The Ravioli Kid

An Original Spaghetti Western

Michelle Freedman

ILLUSTRATED BY
Jason Abbott

Gibbs Smith, Publisher
Salt Lake City

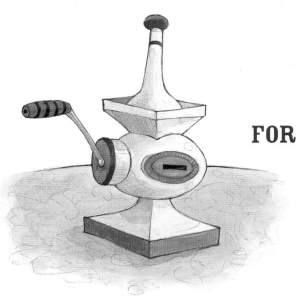

FOR LILIANA,
THE MAESTRO OF MACARONI—MF

FOR MELISSA—JA

First Edition
09 08 07 06 05   5 4 3 2 1

Text © 2005 Michelle Freedman
Illustrations © 2005 Jason Abbott

Published by
Gibbs Smith, Publisher
P.O. Box 667
Layton, Utah 84041

Orders: 1.800 748.5439
www.gibbs-smith.com

Designed by Dawn DeVries Sokol
Printed and bound in Hong Kong

Library of Congress Cataloging-in-Publication Data

Freedman, Michelle.
    The Ravioli Kid : an original spaghetti western / Michelle
Freedman ; illustrations by Jason Abbott. -- 1st ed.
        p. cm.
    Summary: Seven-year-old Stellina Pomodoro must rescue her
parents' "ristorante" and the entire town of El Pasta, using an
unorthodox method to capture the Anti-Pasta gang.
    ISBN 1-58685-438-0
    [1. Pasta products--Fiction. 2. Humorous stories.]   I. Abbott,
Jason, 1972-   , ill. II. Title.
PZ7.F87284Rav 2005
[Fic]--dc22
                                                2005007937

Stellina could not remember a time when the badlands were good. Each of the seven years she had lived there, something terrible had happened.

When she was one, the pasta dough would not divide.

During her second year, all the plum tomatoes spoiled and tasted like lemons.

At age three, everyone in town fell ill from eating bad anchovies.

Her mother lost the
fourth cheese for the
Quattro Formaggio festival
when she was four.

The chickens refused
to lay eggs when
she was five.

And the winter of six
was so cold the pasta
water wouldn't boil.

Out of all the bad things that
had happened in the badlands,
it appeared seven was going to be
her worst year yet. Seven was the
year Angel Hair and his Gang of
Anti-Pasta came to town.

Angel Hair was as mean as he was bad. His long stringy hair was always sticking with the olive oil that oozed from his pitted complexion. He roamed the badlands with his cohorts Pauroso and Marinato, the Gemelli brothers. They found trouble wherever they looked.

Pauroso had an appetite as enormous as his thick belly. He wore diamond-studded olives on his fingertips and shirts stained with marinara sauce.

Marinato constantly picked his teeth with a porcupine quill. He shed his skin like a rattlesnake and wore it around the crown of his dusty fedora.

Angel Hair had gotten wind of golden wheat fields in a town called El Pasta. The three bandits set out to make it their own.

The wind whistled a foreboding tune as the
Anti-Pasta Gang followed the Rioletti Grande
in the direction of El Pasta.

Stellina looked out the kitchen window and watched the golden wheat sway in the wind. She had heard the wind whistle the same tune six times before. She knew it could only mean one thing: Trouble was on the way.

Stellina's parents, Angelo and Felinna Pomodoro, ran Rosa's, a "ristorante" on Main Street, El Pasta, right next to Mr. Cappelletti's Haberdashery.

The Pomodoros made all the pasta served at Rosa's from scratch. The wheat they grew gave it a beautiful golden color.

ROSA'S

WINE:
MERLOT   CHABLIS
CHARDONNAY   CHAMPAGNE
CHIANTI

"GOLDEN" SPECIALS:
RAVIOLI w/ MARINARA $4
MANICOTTI w/ PESTO $4
BAKED ZITI $3

ENTREES:
SPAGHETTI w/ RED SAUCE $3
FETTICINI ALFREDO $3
VERMICELLI $2
LASAGNA $4

Mrs. Pomodoro always mixed and divided the dough, and Mr. Pomodoro always rolled and shaped it into strips.

Stellina's job was to sprinkle the dough with golden flour

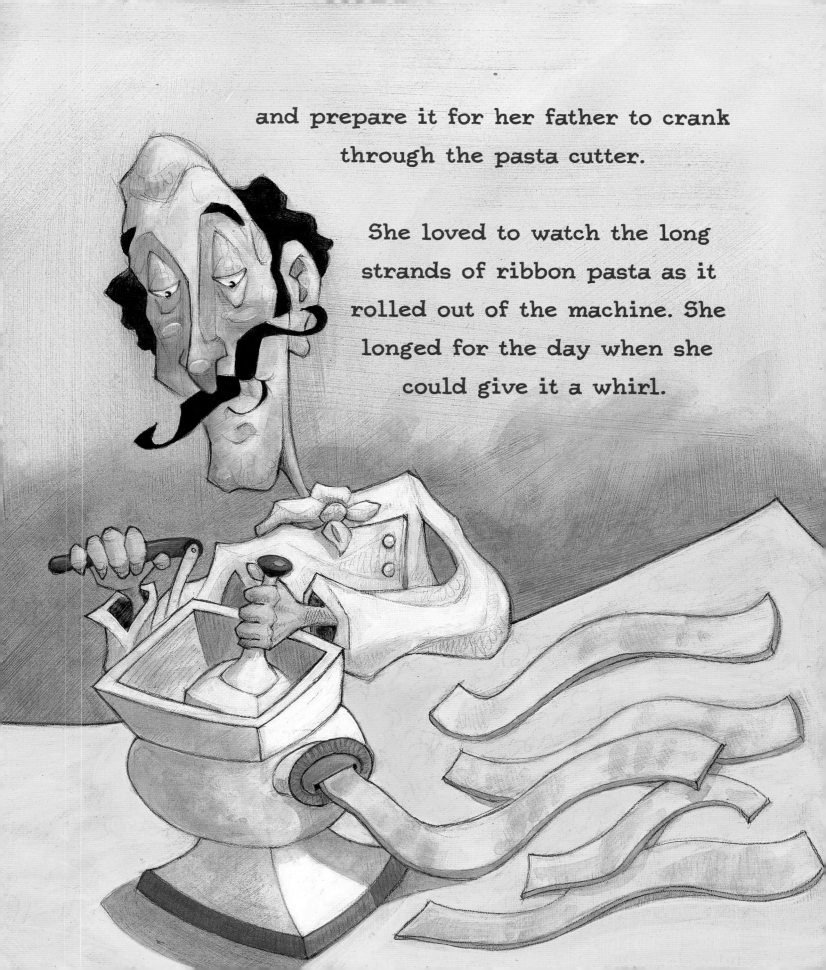

and prepare it for her father to crank
through the pasta cutter.

She loved to watch the long
strands of ribbon pasta as it
rolled out of the machine. She
longed for the day when she
could give it a whirl.

Late summer was
wheat harvest time in El
Pasta. The Pomodoros decided to make golden
ravioli for the harvest festival.

Mrs. Pomodoro mixed and divided the dough and prepared it
for Stellina to sprinkle with the golden flour.

The sacks of flour were kept in the barn behind Rosa's. Stellina walked between the rows of pasta that were hung out to dry. They swayed in the wind like a horse's mane.

Suddenly, the wind was quiet and
the wheat was still.

The sacks of flour had been looted!

Stellina ran back to the kitchen as fast as she could, but it was too late. Angel Hair and the Anti-Pasta Gang had gotten there first. They were greedily stashing the golden ravioli into their loot bags.

The Gemelli brothers had locked
Mr. and Mrs. Pomodoro in the
pantry. Angel Hair had plans to
lock Stellina in there too!

Stellina knew she had but one chance to save El Pasta
from Angel Hair and the Anti-Pasta Gang.

She reached for the crank on the pasta machine and turned it. It was heavier than she expected. With all her might, she fed the dough through the cutter and rolled out long strands of spaghetti.

She quickly fashioned a lasso with the noodles, ducking to avoid getting hit with the pasta shells that were flying across the kitchen. This was the worst food fight anyone had ever seen!

Stellina whistled loudly to get the Anti-Pasta Gang's attention. As they headed wildly toward her, she swung the spaghetti high over her head. She aimed, threw, and roped them together into a "cannelloni-alla-outlaw" bundle!

Everyone in Rosa's cheered! Stellina had captured the
Anti-Pasta Gang single-handedly.

Just then a mysterious stranger appeared in the doorway.

He freed Mr. and Mrs. Pomodoro from the pantry and tied
the outlaws to the back of his horse. As he left
he turned to Stellina and said, "There are
two kinds of people in the world, my
friend—those with spaghetti around their
neck, and those who have the job of
doing the cutting."

The next day at the harvest festival,
Sheriff Tom Mixta awarded Stellina a medal of honor.

On it was engraved "The Ravioli Kid."

SPAGHETTI WESTERNS are a type of movie made in Italy in the 1960s and 1970s. They are called "spaghetti westerns" because the movies are set in the old American West (westerns), but they were made in Italy (spaghetti). One of the best-known directors of these films was named Sergio Leone. He directed the famous cowboy actor Clint Eastwood and used the unforgettable music composed by Ennio Morricone in his most famous films.

ABOUT THE PASTA

Angel Hair is a thin, long pasta known as "capellini" in Italian. The character Angel Eyes (played by Lee Van Cleef) appeared in Sergio Leone's film The Good, the Bad, and the Ugly in 1966.

Anti-Pasta, in Italian "antipasto," is an appetizer eaten before the pasta course.

Cannelloni are thin, rectangular sheets of pasta wrapped around a variety of fillings. Cannelloni means "large reeds" in Italian.

Cappelletti is a type of stuffed pasta. In Italian it means "little hats." "Capello" is the Italian word for cowboy hat. A "fedora" is another type of hat.

Gemelli is the Italian word for "twins." It is also a type of dried pasta.

Marinato is Italian for "pickled" or "marinated."

Pasta is from the Italian word for "paste," meaning a combination of flour and water.

Pauroso is Italian for "coward." It literally means "chicken."

Pomodoro is Italian for "tomato."

Quattro formaggio is Italian for "four cheese."

Ravioli is a pasta that gets its name from the verb "to wrap."

Stellina is from "stellini," a variety of "pastina" (little pasta) which means "little stars." They are often used in children's dishes and soups.

HLOOX +
E
FREED

FREEDMAN, MICHELLE
THE RAVIOLI KID

LOOSCAN
07/06